STAR WARS
THE
MANDALORIAN
THE PATH OF THE FORCE

WRITTEN BY
BROOKE VITALE

ILLUSTRATED BY
TOMATOFARM

Disney
LUCASFILM
P R E S S
Los Angeles • New York

Mando was on a quest.
He had been tasked with
taking the Child to a Jedi.

But to find a Jedi,
he needed help from
another Mandalorian.

On Tatooine, Mando met a man.
He wore Mandalorian armor.
But he was not a Mandalorian.

The man's name was Cobb Vanth.
He wanted Mando's help
to kill a krayt dragon.
As thanks, he gave Mando his
armor.

Mando still needed
to find other Mandalorians.
Mando met a sailor who said
he knew where to find some.

Mando went with the sailor.
But it was a trap.
He pushed the Child into a tank.
Mando dove in after him.

The sailor locked the tank.
Mando tried to get free,
but he could not.
Out of nowhere,
three Mandalorians appeared.
They saved Mando and the Child.

Their leader was Bo-Katan.
She wanted Mando's help.
If he did what she asked,
she would help him find a Jedi.

Mando helped her take control of an enemy ship.
Bo kept her word. She told Mando to go to the planet Corvus.

On Corvus, Mando could find
a Jedi named Ahsoka Tano.
Mando wanted to go right away.
But his ship was broken.

Mando took his ship to an old friend.

Greef Karga was happy to see Mando.

He would fix the ship.

But he needed Mando's help to destroy an old base of the Empire's.

Inside the base, Mando found a lab.

There was a message from Moff Gideon.

Moff Gideon was still alive!

And he still wanted the Child.

Mando had to find the Jedi.
He set off at once.
But as he looked for Ahsoka,
she attacked.

Then the Jedi saw the Child.
She stopped fighting.
Mando watched as she spoke to
him.
She learned his name was Grogu.

Ahsoka tried to test Grogu's
power.
But he was too scared.
He would not use his power.

Ahsoka asked Mando to try.
Mando held out a ball.
Slowly, Grogu used his power.

Ahsoka told Mando about an old temple.
It was strong in the Force.
He was to take Grogu there.

Grogu was too attached to
Mando.
Ahsoka could not train him.
Grogu would have to choose his
own path.

Mando took Grogu to the temple.

He set him down.

He waited.

But nothing happened.

Just then, Mando heard a ship.
He reached for Grogu.
A wave of power threw him back.
Grogu was using the Force.

The ship's pilot was Boba Fett!
He wanted the armor
Cobb had given to Mando.
It was his.

If Mando gave him the armor,
Boba Fett would protect the
Child.
But it was too late.
Moff Gideon's dark troopers had
taken Grogu!

Mando had to find Moff Gideon
and save Grogu.
He could not do it alone.
He needed help from an old
enemy.

The two found Moff Gideon's ship.
But they ran into a problem.
Mando had to take off his helmet.
He had to show his face.

On Moff Gideon's ship,
Mando found Grogu.
Moff Gideon was with him.
He held the Darksaber over
Grogu.

Moff Gideon attacked Mando.

Mando fought back.

He won.

The Darksaber was his.

Just then, an alarm went off.

Dark troopers were attacking.

A man appeared.

He fought the dark troopers.

Grogu sensed him.

Mando opened the door.
The man walked in.
He took off his hood.
It was Luke Skywalker!

Mando knew this was the Jedi
he had been looking for.
Mando told Grogu
to go with the Jedi.

Grogu touched Mando's helmet.
Mando took off the helmet.
For the first time,
Grogu saw his friend's face.

Mando watched as Grogu went
with the Jedi.
He had completed his quest.
Grogu was where he belonged.